Playing Slot Machines

Anthony Crafts

ISBN: 9781521501573

DEDICATION

I dedicate this book to my awesome parents, Mark and Sue; also my high roller brother, Charles and my sweet sister, Rachel. Of course I can't forget my nephew Scotty and my nieces Natalie and Allison.

CONTENTS

ACKNOWLEDGMENTS

I would like to thank Aaron, Alec, Bryce, Jon and Tyler for coming to the casino with me at all hours and for telling me all their game play secrets and also Walt for proof reading the final version.

1 PICK THE RIGHT CASINO

Some casinos have better overall odds than others. Why? Well, it depends on a few things, but mostly it boils down to one question. How does the casino attract gamblers? The ultimate goal of any casino owner or manager is to bring people in. The more people playing, typically the more profitable the casino will be. Some casinos attract people using shows, inexpensive food, free drinks, etc.... I usually stay away from these places. Unless they have a strong reputation for good odds, I avoid the big, fancy establishments. It's simple economics. If a waitress is serving free drinks to players, that's an extra cost to the casino. They need to make up the difference somewhere, and since the players are drinking they probably won't notice the win/loss ratio as much. So, the casino makes it very hard to win.

When I am deciding on a casino to play

at, I want to know a few things first. Is the casino regulated? Believe it or not many casinos are unregulated and are not required to report to any government agency. They can make the odds of winning absolutely impossible, and sometimes they do! Modern technology gives the managers the ability to change the odds on a single machine, a group of machines, or the entire casino. It could be as simple as clicking a button on a computer or it might even be fully automated. The managers can increase or decrease the odds of winning anytime they want. Some casinos are even setup to change the odds automatically during certain times of day and/or days of the week. It's also possible for the system to detect how many players are in the casino and change the odds of winning based on how full or empty the floor is.

Casinos that are regulated by the state are less risky than unregulated casinos, but the payoff might be less. Playing in an unregulated casino is kind of like playing the stock market back in the late 90's during all the deregulation that went on.

The risk goes up, but the payoff can be high as well. If you decide to play at an unregulated casino it's very important to do some research and speak with some regular players. Also, it doesn't hurt to walk up to someone who is already playing and ask "Is it a lucky night?" Or "Which machines are paying out big?" I do it all the time, nobody's ever been offended. I've gotten some useful information this way. Now, if someone tells me it's a lucky night and there have been lots of payouts all over the floor, I will verify this before jumping in. Talking to players just gives me a good initial idea of what kind of night it's going to be. I sometimes talk to the staff as well. They know what's going on better than anyone. This can be a little trickier though. Some casinos tell their employees not to give any advice to the players.

Now, if a casino is unregulated, and therefore a little riskier, that doesn't mean I automatically avoid it. It just means I need to change my game plan a little. I actually like unregulated casinos. I simply want to know which kind I'm dealing with ahead of time. If it's a regulated casino I'm not going to spend as much time trying to detect fluctuations in the odds. I will spend more time finding the area or machine that looks right for me. How do you find out if a casino is regulated? Just ask. Or many times you can find the information on the Internet.

Once I've established whether or not the casino is regulated by the state, another thing I want to know is how long the casino has been open. A newer casino might be struggling to attract patrons. If the managers don't have the budget for headline shows or free drinks they might decide to increase the odds of winning, and possibly keep it that way for an extended period of time. Once word gets out, their casino might be full of regular players, then they can make it harder to win again.

The size of the casino can also be a determining factor. Sometimes the small, truck stop casino with 100 machines or less has better odds than the bigger counterparts. It's not always the case, so be sure to do some research before sitting down to a machine. I will discuss how to do that in later chapters. The smaller casinos are usually out of the way, not near any major city attractions so the best way for them to attract new players is to keep the odds of winning higher. They are usually attached to a gas station or hotel so the casino isn't their only source of revenue. They can afford a slightly smaller slot machine profit margin if it means attracting more customers overall.

How full is the casino? Is that a factor? I've heard various opinions on this subject and I have no real proof either way, but personally, I think odds are better when there are fewer people playing. Look at it from the casino owner's perspective. If the casino is packed why make the odds better to win? Alternately, if the casino is empty the managers might be panicking, trying to think of ways to generate publicity.

In summary, if I find a smaller, perk less, recently constructed, unregulated casino with a near empty parking lot I'm there baby!

2 GET PREPARED

Ok! So, you've found the perfect casino and you're about to walk in and sit down the first machine that catches your eye. Don't! Instead, take a minute. You're not in any hurry. First, what's the money situation? Do you have a hundred dollar bill and a fifty? Big mistake! You shouldn't have anything bigger than a ten, hopefully, lots of ones. This is something I am going to talk about a lot in future chapters but the truth is you can sometimes be your own worst enemy. I see so many people feed a hundred dollar bill into a machine like it's nothing, then just start hitting buttons, or worse yet the same button over and over. They go into some kind of trance and then suddenly, their money is gone. Well, of course! If you're going to play that way you might as well just go up the cashier, hand over whatever money you have in your pockets, and be done with it. When you first walk into a casino you've got to go into detective mode. It's your job to find out which machines are paying. I adhere to a simple principle when playing the slots. A machine that is paying is likely to keep paying. On the flipside of that though a machine that is not paying (or being greedy as I like to call it) is likely to stay that way. Not forever, just for the time being. Don't make the mistake of writing off a machine forever. I've been burned by a machine and then later had it pay off for me, it just depends on the day, or maybe even the time of day.

I recently visited a local casino with my brother Charles. He lost several hundred dollars very quickly and even though he was frustrated he just shrugged it off and said "It's no big deal." If I lost that much that quick I'd be in the alley crying. To be honest this was very unusual. Charles is someone who I consider to be "naturally lucky". He has the attitude "Go big or go home" and I will say, it usually pays off for him. If you are that type of person, congratulations! The rest of us will need to rely on strategizing to win.

So, after you've turned those big bills into singles, fives, and tens (mostly singles) the next thing you want to do is look around. Wow! What an idea, right? Sounds simple, but there are a few things you want to pay attention too. How full is the casino? More than half empty? Is it packed? I like a casino that's more on the empty side. The fewer people the better. I just imagine the casino managers saying to each other "Hey, we need to attract people. Let's make the odds of winning better." Even if that isn't actually happening I am convinced that odds of winning are controlled remotely. But, even if the casino is packed, it's not a deal breaker. You just need to be a little more careful and do a little more detective work. Now, walk up and down some aisles. Pay attention to the screens. Look at the total credits. As you walk around are you seeing high numbers or low? If you see lots of high numbers that can be a good sign. It either means people are feeding large amounts into the machines (bad mistake) or it means they are winning money. Hopefully, it's the latter. Next, find a spot kind of in the middle of the floor. Just stand there for a minute or two. At this point, you might be attracting the attention of the security team, but oh well, you're a detective and you have a job to do. Stand there and look around. Take a full 360. Do you hear or see any machines making a big payout? If you notice several machines flashing and making all kinds of noise that can definitely be a good sign! Especially if the casino is less than half full. This means they have probably increased the odds of winning on the floor. They actually want people to win. Most people who win big at the casino end up giving that money back to the casino by staying longer than they should. I know people who simply refuse to leave unless their pockets are completely empty. It's foolish, I will talk more about this later but one of the most important things to know when playing slots is when to leave. If the managers have increased the odds of winning for the time being this might be a great time to take advantage. But, before you hop on any machine there are a few more things to do. Let's talk to some people. Get over that awkward shyness and just walk up to somebody. Wait, not that guy. He looks like a serial killer. Let's find someone else. Over there, the guy in the purple. Ask him if it's been a lucky night and if they have seen lots of big wins. Go on! When a machine is winning big it attracts a lot of attention. When I ask people can usually tell me the machine, how much the player won, and about how long ago it was. If they tell you it's a lucky night that's a good sign. If they say "Get out while you still can" then take a mental note. Ask more than one person, at least three. Ok, so now it's time to decide if you are going to stay at this casino. You might be thinking "Hey Anthony, I just got here. No way am I just going to walk out." If all signs show that it's going to be a bad night then don't be afraid to walk away. You can always come back another day. If you've done your detective work and you feel comfortable and maybe even confident then it's time to continue to the next steps.

3 KNOW THINE ENEMY

When playing slot machines you have two primary enemies. Your first enemy is the casino owners. They want you to spend money, and enjoy doing it. Everything in the casino is set up for just that purpose. Your second enemy is yourself! That's right, you can be your own worst enemy when it comes to playing slots. Let's talk about the casino first. Casinos of today are very different from those of the past, Slot machines especially! A modern slot machine is really just a computer and it can be networked with all the slot machines in the building. It can also be linked with other machines in other casinos around the world. This enables the casino owners to control everything about that machine remotely. The odds of winning could be completely changed while you are playing and you would never know it unless you know what to look for.

Why would the casino owners want to change the odds of winning? Well, look at it from their perspective. Maybe there is some special event nearby, or it's a holiday and so now you have a completely packed casino. Wouldn't you want to capitalize on that event? Of course you would! Let me tell you a story. I used to work at a gas station. We knew that we were just about the only place open on Christmas morning and because we had been open in years past we knew that our store would be flooded with customers looking for batteries for all the new Christmas toys. So you know what we did? Late November, we ordered an absolutely insane number of batteries. We had them stocked in the back room, the refrigerator, we even put some in the bathroom. And then on Christmas morning we changed the price of all batteries in the store. Do you think we lowered the price? No, we doubled it. And not only did we sell out, we sold out fast! By noon on Christmas day we were out of every battery in the store and we still had customers coming in looking for more. You might be wondering why I'm telling you this story. Because, casinos are the same way. If they know their casino is going to be packed with people they are going to try to make as much money off that as possible. They don't even have to try to win anyone over. They just let the money flow in. Now, when the event or holiday is over that's when it's time to make the odds of winning a little "friendlier". Back to business as usual. That's why I don't like to see a casino that's completely packed. I know the casino managers have lowered the chances of winning to make the most money.

My friend Matt is also my manager at work. He is awesome. Nobody lives life to the fullest quite like him. I am content to sleep a day away. That would be a criminal act in his mind. He and I were actually going to start a blog on ways to manage finances properly, which is why he was a little surprised when I told him I was going to start playing the slot machines. I don't thing Matt would ever put a single penny into a slot machine. He would consider it a complete waste of money, and that's ok. Everyone has a different opinion when it comes to playing slot machines. Not everyone finds it amusing and entertaining like I do.

Now, there's nothing you can do to stop the casino from altering the odds of winning. But sometimes, just being aware of it is a powerful tool. With this knowledge I'm much less likely to get stuck on a machine that has gone cold, or is not paying out spin after spin. I'm able to tell myself – "Hey, they've changed the odds. This is not working out. Time to find another machine."

A couple of years ago I visited Jackpot, Nevada with friends from work, Bryce, Zach, and Devin. We actually got caught in a huge snow storm and had to stay overnight unexpectedly. The next day they all told me that I take snoring to a whole new level, but that's beside the point. Zach won't have anything to do with slot machines. He likes to play cards and I have no problem with that. To each their own, right? So, he was in another room for a tournament while Bryce, Devin and I took to the floor. Bryce did something that I think is a good idea. He gave most of his money to Zach to help him manage it so he didn't spend too much at once. I do this myself sometimes and I've been glad I did. By the time I find the person and wrestle more money away from them I've usually come to my senses and I am ready to hit the dinner buffet.

Casinos have many ways to trick you into making common mistakes. There's a lot going on that the average player isn't aware of. For example, there could be certain areas of the casino that attract more customers. Some people like to sit by a door or window. Others might feel more comfortable sitting close to a restroom. You never know. But, the casino knows. They keep track of everything and then transform that data into useful information. They then use that information to make decisions, like what the odds for winning should be on a particular machine.

Everything from the color of the ceiling,

to the pattern on the carpet, to the distance between each machine has been carefully chosen to make you want to gamble. They have sophisticated techniques used to herd us around like cattle. That's why it's up to us to be smart and well informed enough to fight against the casino and take as much as we can. Believe me, they don't feel bad about taking your money, so don't feel bad about taking theirs.

4 MAKE A PLAN

I used to watch "The A Team" every day after school. Hannibal used to say "I love it when a plan comes together". Well, this is just like an episode of "The A Team" and we are gunna make a plan of attack.

Now that we've found our perfect casino and we are more aware of the tricks the casino is going to try to use against us we are ready to prepare our plan of attack.

First, I like to pull a few singles out of my wallet and tell myself "this is throw away money". I'm not playing the slots yet, I'm just testing the waters. I want to get some idea of how friendly the odds might be. I find three or four machines in opposite parts of the floor. It's easy to do, even in small casinos – just pick the four corners to make it easy. Play one or two dollars at each machine. You don't need to bet a lot – just pennies or nickels.

Remember, you're not playing yet, just testing the water.

When I told my friend Walt I was going to the casino regularly he laughed. Walt plays the slots every once in a while, but it's no big deal to him. He is an artist and has many interests. Slot play just isn't enough to really pull him in and that's ok. As a matter of fact I would rather see a friend have too little interest in slots than too much. It's good to have some friends that are not really interested because they can tell you if you are getting out of control.

Pretend like you are a scientist doing a study of some sort. There are several things you want to pay attention to. How many times in a row did you spin without winning anything? How many times do you bonus? How many times do you have a win that is ten or more times your average bet? Just keep track of this. Make a mental note. You don't have to be writing anything down, it's enough to just be aware of these things – then after fifty spins or so you'll be able to make a good judgement as to how friendly the machine is. Just ask yourself, on a scale from one to ten, the higher the better – how lucky is this machine? If you find the machine is lucky and paying out stay on it. It's ok. You can pick up the investigative work later. Go ahead and play this for a while. Just be careful and pay close attention to winning and losing trends. Don't risk a lot on this machine. When you are done having fun get back to the investigation.

My friend Alec is a season professional when it comes to playing the slots. He really knows what he's doing and it is fun to watch. He follows all the rules and he has a great natural instinct when it comes to knowing what machines to play and how much to bet on each spin. If I'm taking a break from the slots, sometimes I will watch him play. It's fun seeing a pro at work.

Now, once you've played at least two or three machines in each area think about what area you were luckiest in. Go back to that area and play at least two more dollars. Remember, just pennies and nickels at this point. If these machines both score lower than a five, start over. It may not sound fun but it can pay off. I've spend a couple of hours investigating and I've never regretted it. If you can't find an area that scores higher than a five on average – guess what, it's time to make like a tree and leave. I know you don't want to, but it's better. Trust me. You'll get to play again another day.

If you find an area that scores higher than five on average then you are ready to pick the perfect machine.

5 THE GHOST IN THE MACHINE

Ever heard of artificial intelligence (AI)? It's very real. It's a very powerful tool with a wide variety of uses. As I mentioned earlier, the casino managers don't need to manually raise and lower the odds of winning. This can all be done automatically at any time and there doesn't even need to be a person making the decision to do so.

The system can be pre-programmed to raise or lower the odds when certain criteria are met. The odds on individual machines can be raised or lowered independently of each other. One machine could have great odds of winning at the moment and the next one could be programmed with lousy odds.

Modern slot machines are not just simple random number generators. I'm not sure when it happened but at some point slot machines got very smart. It's almost like there is a person in there controlling everything. Not really, but it's better to err on the side of caution. I had a college professor that always used to say "The question isn't whether you should be paranoid. The question is are you paranoid enough?" He was talking mostly about cyber security, but the same question applies here. When you are playing slots you better bet you are being watched, and not just by the security cameras. That machine is programmed to keep track of everything you do, including how long you take between spins, how often you change your bet, your average, high, and low bets. If you came from another machine and used a printed ticket it brings over all the data from the previous machine.

Now, what does it do with all this data? A whole lot! Casino owners have a tremendous knowledge of basic human psychology. They use it to make all kinds of decisions like how bright the ceiling lights should be, to what type of chairs to put in front of each slot machine. Everything is orchestrated to keep you playing. Well, all that knowledge they have can be programmed into a computer. That slot machine can tell if you are losing interest in it based on a variety of factors. It can how desperate you are to win. It can tell if you are probably going to be playing at this machine for a while, or if you are about done. It can even make a very good guess as to how much money you have with you and what you are going to bet next. All of this information can be used against you psychologically to manipulate you into betting higher and staying longer.

Scared? Well, don't be. Even the most advanced artificial intelligence or AI systems have limitations, and the best defense you have against them is knowledge. Once you know what they are looking for, it's easy to trick them. The more you learn about AI the more you begin to recognize the decisions that are being made behind the scenes. The most modern machines have very advance AI built in. It is spectacular and that's one of the many reasons I avoid newer, fancier machines. I'll discuss this more in the next chapter but I always look for the older machines to play first.

Once you have played the same machine over and over that particular machine almost starts to develop a personality. And, that's not too far from the truth because it was probably programmed with a basic personality, or the AI equivalent. For example, there is one machine I frequent that falls for the same trick every

That brings me to my next subject, Player's Club Cards. Don't use them! I know. You want the points and the free stuff. It's actually not worth it and I will explain why.

Don't let the system track you. If you win some money, cash out. Then turn your ticket into singles. You can go right back to the same machine – and the system thinks you are a different player.

6 PICK THE RIGHT MACHINE

Now that you have the area of the casino narrowed down, it's time to pick the right machine.

Another thing casinos commonly do is lure people in with themes. Hey, I love Gilligan's Island just as much as they next guy, but that doesn't mean I have to play the skipper's slot machine. Don't be fooled by expensive advertising. When I look around a casino I try to imagine a room full of plain, beige desktop PC's from the late 90's. You know the ones with the huge CRT monitors. Because that's all they really are. When I see a fifteen foot tall machine with a dazzling display, you know what I do? I move on. No thanks. It doesn't impress me, because I know behind all the bells, whistles and flashing lights it's just a desktop PC, exactly like the one sitting next to it. But, the casino had to pay big bucks for that new fancy machine and they want to get their money's worth.

I try to find the oldest machine in the casino. I want the one that's been on the floor since the early 90's. Maybe the staff even has a nickname for it. It's kind of slow. The screen is dim. The speakers glitch out every once in a while. Dust is collecting on it because nobody has played it in quite some time. That's my buddy, right there. I love this guy. I just want to give him a big hug! This is where I start.

Sometimes you can find a whole row of them. Or maybe even a whole room full. If you can, and it's in an area that has tested well from the steps you took in the previous chapter, then you are really in luck. This is the type of area I can spend hours and hours in.

So, aside from finding the older

machines, I also like to look for a machine that has had a recent big win. Just walk up and down the aisles and look at the screens. Most games will show you what the last person bet and won. If you see a good ratio (small bet, big win) sit down and play a few spins. Don't risk a whole lot, maybe just start with pennies or nickels. Try to get an idea of how the machine is performing.

My buddy Aaron had never played the slot machines before. I was with him the first time he tried. It was like watching a

Find a machine that is in the middle of the room. The casino wants to publicize big wins. A machine making a lot of winning noises in the middle of the casino is always good for business, so casinos are likely to make the machines in the middle win more. Also, look for a machine that is being worked on by the casino staff. Maybe they are emptying the safe inside or possibly making a repair. If they are just getting done and making the machine ready for game play again I'd put a few dollars in and give it a whirl. Once they open the door to the machine it resets. It's possible the first few spins after being reset could be very lucky.

down to their last few credits. They weren't paying attention.

That's not the way you are going to play. Ever. Promise me. Maybe you did that in the past, but no more. My buddy Aaron is the best example of how to keep your head in the game. He is constantly changing his bet, stopping the spin, he is very involved in everything that is going on. That's the way we all should be. We've already discussed all the different ways these machines keep track of every movement made by the player. Believe me, once you zone out and just start hitting the button like you are working on some kind of assembly line, the machine knows it, and it's likely been programmed to lower the odds of winning. It's almost like the machine is saying "Hey, you aren't paying attention, so why don't I just take everything."

I told tanner I about this book and asked him what advice he wants to give the readers. He gave me an incredible piece of advice that I'm surprised I didn't think of on my own. He said "Never play angry."

It's so true. If you aren't having fun then what's the point. Don't forget, slot play is a game and games are supposed to be fun. If you are getting overly frustrated, take a break.

If you feel your mind wandering or you start slipping into a slot machine trance one thing you can do is up your bet a little higher than normal. Nothing too extreme, just enough to scare yourself. Get that adrenaline pumping again! Then you can go back down to a normal bet. If you really can't snap out of it you might be bored. Take a break from slots or try a different machine. Sometimes I go watch a friend play for a little while. About ten minutes of that and I'm ready to get right back into the game with full verve.

So, back to the title of the chapter – Alcohol is absolutely out of the question. No way! Why do you think some casinos offer free alcohol while you play? It's not to be hospitable. They know you are much more likely to stop caring if you've had a drink or two. If you are going to succeed at slot play you've got to have your head in the game at all times.

8 IT'S GO TIME! – GAME PLAY

Oh my goodness. We're almost at the end of the book and we haven't had a single spin! I remember a college professor telling a story the first day of class. Well, not so much a story as it is an analogy. Anyway, here it goes. Imagine you are in the military and you need to get from your current location to a safe house just across the street. Everyone can see the destination from the window, but the commander tells you to take an indirect route. He wants all of us to go clear across town and then back again to avoid snipers. Well, most of the group say to themselves – "That's silly, I can see the safe house from here." And they make a run for it. A few people actually follow the commander's instructions. Guess who makes it safely across the street. That's right, the ones that took the indirect route. If you run into a casino and sit right down to the first machine that catches your eye, you are doomed to fall for every trick the casino has set up. If you take your time and do some preliminary work, you will be much happier with the results.

Now, where are we? Oh yea, we've found the perfect casino, best area of the casino, and even the right machine. Here we are, just the two of us. Could you scoot over a little? Thanks. All our hard work has brought us to this single point. Ahhhh. Take a minute to reflect. Pat yourself on the back.

Ok, now what?

Now is a good time to think about what kind of player you are. There are varying degrees of what I call seriousness. There's no right or wrong here, just a question. Why do you play slot machines? The answer is going to help us formulate your best strategy for game play.

When I told my parents I was going to take up slot machine gambling as a hobby they didn't jump around the room for joy. At first they were a bit puzzled. I remember them saying "That's not like you." But as I explained to them that it was just a form of entertainment like going to the movies or visiting an amusement park they realized I wasn't going to be doing anything dangerous. They just told me to be careful. When does slot play become a problem? Well, I'm not a psychologist but my personal opinion is that gambling of any form becomes a problem when it starts impacting other areas of your life, especially areas that are necessary to live happily. If your life is suddenly all about the casino and you spend most of your waking moments trying to get there, then I would say it's time to take break. Maybe a long one. It's ok. Those machines are not going anywhere. Take some time to put things back into perspective before you return to the slots.

Think of a scale from one to ten. Number one is someone who just plays for fun. They don't really care about winning, they have a gambling budget set aside every month and they don't care if they lose every penny of it. They view playing the slot machines the same way they view

going to the movies, or going out to dinner. Pay a fee, have some fun, that's it.

Now, moving up the scale to number five we have someone who enjoys playing, but also enjoys winning. This person doesn't like going home empty handed, but also isn't planning on depending on slot machine winnings to support himself.

Finally, all the way up to number ten. This is the most serious player of all. This person considers slot play to be their retirement plan. They are either going to win big and retire, or win consistently enough to make slot play their regular job.

Thinking about this scale, where are you? As I mentioned, there is no right or wrong here, just different people with different interests. This book can be used by any slot player at any point on the scale, but each person will use the book differently.

The next steps I outline in this chapter can be used at varying degrees. If you are lower on the scale, say a two or three then you can be less strict about following these next steps. I still want you to follow the investigative work in the previous chapters, because I mean, hey, who doesn't like to win?

If you score higher on the scale this is where things really get serious for you. I want you to pay careful attention to every small detail in the rest of this chapter and follow each step exactly.

Believe it or not, the first thing I think about when sitting down to a machine is moving to another machine. "What?" you say. "That doesn't make any sense." Sure it does. Think about it. This machine is on probation. I start out very suspicious, ready to leave at any second. If it doesn't dazzle me right away, I'm leaving. There are plenty of other machines to play on.

First make sure you have plenty of singles in your wallet. This is your secret weapon against the artificial intelligence you are combating against. Put in a single dollar bill and start playing the lowest bet possible. For me it's usually a penny since

I like penny machines. Make about thirty spins and then sit back and think. Let's take a mental inventory. How did the machine do? Are you up? Are you down thirty cents? Did you bonus? How many spins did you go in a row without winning anything at all? As you are asking yourself these questions rate the machine on a scale from one to ten (one being the worst). If the machine scores a one to four move on. Don't waste your time. If it's a five, six or seven – flip a coin. It's up to you. If it gets a score of eight or above it's time to get serious. Put some more money in and move the bet up the next increment. Make about thirty more spins. Evaluate the machine again and then go on from there.

If a machine seems to be treating me ok and I've decided to spend some time at it I like to change my bet around. I'm not going to just sit there and hit the fifty cent spin over and over mindlessly. The machines love it when we do that because it means we are in some kind of trance and not really thinking about what we are doing. I mix it up. I will bet low for a while, then high, then middle ground. I try to make it as random as possible.

I also like to change the amount of time I wait between spins. Yes, the artificial intelligence (A.I) is timing how long it takes you to press the button again and it can use that information against you. I will hit the button almost immediately after each spin finishes for a while, then I will wait about ten seconds between each spin. Sometimes I will stop, check my phone, take a sip of soda and look around between each spin. I like to drive that A.I. crazy.

If I have a fairly large win, say twenty dollars or more, I will cash out. That's right, I take the little print out up to the teller and get cash. Small bills. Then I will come back and start over with a single dollar again. Now the machine thinks it's lost a player and it needs to do even better to keep the next player around longer.

The A.I. will try to lure you in with a decent win just to get your blood pumping. Then it will put you on a losing streak until you are down to zero. I've seen it happen over and over. You see that win and you think another one is right around the corner. – Ok, maybe it is. But you need to limit the number of chances you will give that machine to give you another decent win. If you go ten or fifteen spins without winning anything cash out and go get a bunch of ones.

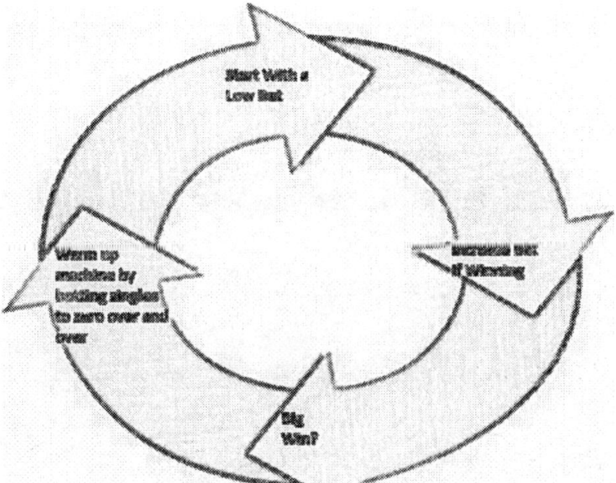

Now, I'm not saying leave the machine

completely, I'm just saying mess with it a little. Show it whose boss. The next step might seem contrary to what I told you before, but the difference is you've determined this is a machine that's worth spending some time on, so let's see if we can win some money. Go back and put a dollar in. Play it all the way to zero. Play whatever increments you want. If you feel like playing for a while, play pennies. Once you've reached zero, wait a moment. Take a sip of your non-alcoholic beverage (better be). Look around. Now, put another dollar in. Play it to zero just like the last one. Do this three or four times. It drives the A.I. crazy. The machine actually thinks its losing players one after another. Its self-esteem is getting lower and lower. Leaving a machine is like leaving a car dealership. They are far more likely to do what you want the second or third time you come back. After a while the machine will do anything to keep the next player around. At this point, go back to playing normally. Put a dollar in, start betting small and slowly work your way up. And yes, I drew those arrows with my mouse. Aren't they pretty?

Some people say it's silly to look for patterns and they might be right when talking about the old style machines that were not completely computerized. Now that the machines are being run by A.I. it might be useful to look for patterns. My buddy Tyler definitely wins more often than most people. He almost has a second sense when it comes to slot machines. He will suddenly get a strong feeling about one particular machine and, guess what? More often than not, that machine will pay off, big! Now, he says he is able to detect patterns and use them to know when to change his bet. He also does what I call spin stopping. I typically don't spin stop, but I don't see how it could hurt. This is where you stop the machine mid-spin. On some machines this can be done by touching the screen. On others, it's done by pressing the spin button mid-spin.

9 GET OUT

Different players have varying opinions on what the single most important skill, talent, or behavior is when playing slot machines. Many say its game play. Not me. I say it's knowing when to get up and leave the casino. And the second most important thing is knowing when to change machines.

The most common mistake I see in any casino, especially while playing slot machines is staying too long. Seriously, I know people that will not leave the casino until their pockets are completely empty. Even if they win thousands of dollars, they will not leave until it's all gone.

Let's talk about a few simple steps to follow that will help you get up and get out when it's appropriate. First, how much money you are taking to the casino with you. That is your slot machine budget for the night. We are going to use it to make some rules ahead of time. To simplify this scenario let's say you have one hundred dollars.

Rule number one, do not leave the casino with less than five percent of what you came in with. Never, never, never let the casino have your last dime. Believe me, even if you have a bad night and lose most of your money, you will feel much better as you drive away if you at least have a few dollars in your pocket. The temptation to keep gambling is incredibly strong, but if you are down to the last five percent of what you came in with, and you have been following the steps in this book you probably should have left a long time ago. Don't let them have that last little bit. It's yours.

Rule number two, take the amount of money you came into the casino with and divide it by three hundred. This is going to be your average bet. That's right, pull out your smart phone and open the calculator app. I can't do this stuff in my head either, so don't be embarrassed. Ok, so if you have a hundred dollars than your average bet should be thirty-three cents. Now, you can go higher or lower, as a matter of fact I hope you are changing your bet regularly. But on average, stay around this number. It gives you a good amount of game play. You didn't just come to the casino to instantly win (although that would be nice) you came to play. Taking spins on a slot machine is fun. It's entertaining. So, make sure you are betting responsibly. That way, even if the worst happens, you still got to enjoy at least three hundred spins.

Here is rule number three. This one is the most difficult to follow. It's made grown men cry (I'm one of them). But if you can follow it, you will be much, much happier about your overall slot machine experience. Take the amount of money you brought with you and multiply it by thirty. This is going to be our maximum wins. "Maximum wins!?!?" you say. "What are you talking about Anthony?" Yep. I said it. Maximum wins. So, why on earth would I want to limit your wins? That seems stupid. Well, let's talk about it. If you came into the casino with a hundred dollar bill and you are up twenty-nine hundred what are the chances that you are going to do any better than that? Actually they are so small they aren't even worth talking about. Take the three thousand and go. It's going to be one of the most difficult things you have ever done, but get out of that casino. You are not thinking clearly. You are not yourself. A chemical called dopamine is coursing through your blood stream right now. It happens whenever a human being wins something significant, like a large amount of money. In this state you will have a very strong desire to keep gambling. Don't try to talk yourself out of it. Don't think. Just leave.

Get in the car and drive far away. Give your body some time to recover from what just happened. It will probably take a few hours (or maybe even a day or two) for that dopamine to leave your system. Go buy yourself a nice dinner. Maybe get that DVD or Video Game you've been wanting. Buy something tangible. Casinos have a way of making us lose all sense of what money is really used for in our regular day to day lives, especially after a big win. Buying something helps put you back into a normal frame of mind. Over time you will start to come out of that trance and when you do you are going to be so happy you left. You've got a large amount of money in your wallet that you can use for, well, whatever. Pay some bills, splurge a little, have fun! You've earned it! You've done one of the most difficult things anyone can do.

When I told my friend Adam that I was

going to start going to the casino to play slot machines he said "But, you know the math. I know you do." Yea, I know the math. The odds are against me winning, in a big way. I get that. But I view slot play as a form of recreation. I budget a certain amount for gambling and I don't go over that. Now I take every precaution to make sure I have every possible chance of winning, but if I've spent my gambling money for the week, I'm done until next week. I think that's a good rule to live by. Just look at it the same as going out to the movies or going to the circus. You pay a fee, enjoy yourself for a few hours and that's it. Now, with slot play there is an added benefit. You might go home rich!

Now, next time you want to go to the casino take a hundred out of that big win and go! Isn't that cool? Now you are playing the slots with the casino's money. It's like every spin is a free spin! Remember to follow all the steps from the beginning, and hopefully you will be going home with pockets full of money again today! You will become a casino's worst nightmare ha-ha. Not, really. Don't worry about them, they'll do just fine.

10 PSYCHICS, MEDIUMS, AND ESP

So you've reached chapter ten, read the chapter title and said to yourself "What? Who is this nut? He believes in ESP?" Well, yes. Not in a religious sense, but I am convinced there are forces in the universe that are difficult to explain and near impossible to measure yet they still exist. And I'm also convinced that our amazing human brain has the ability to tap into these forces, even if it is to a limited extent. Do I think that psychics can always predict when a machine is going to pay out big? No. If that were the case there would be no casinos. But if you have some ability that might help you make an extra hundred dollars or so every once in a while, or perhaps keep you from making a decision that results in a big loss – well? Good for you! Use it! Hone that ability and make it pay off for you as much as possible.

Now, I know people who are sensitive to these impressions or helpful guidance, they typically call themselves psychics or mediums. They have explained to me that within most groups of people who have these abilities, using them to make money in a casino, or lottery, or even the stock market is generally looked down upon. Look, I'm not trying to persuade anyone to do anything that makes them feel